A Merry Hengrouse Christmas

Lamorna Ireland

AUTHOR

A cosy, festive short story for the readers of Unexpected Beginnings wanting to return to the warmth of Trengrouse Cider Farm at the most magical time of the year.

'This Christmas Short Story will hug you like a warm mug of mulled wine.'

'A truly festive treat with old friends in familiar settings!'

Also By Lamorna Ireland

Lamorna would love to hear from you. Find her on:

Facebook.com/LamornaIreland

@AuthorIreland

www.LamornaIreland.co.uk

To One & All, a very Merry Christmas

Eleven Days Until Christmas...

'Left. Left. Emily, I said left!'

'Oh my god, Sarah. Maybe you should be the one up this rickety old ladder, huh?'

Emily chuckled, shaking her head in amusement before pinning the end of the garland to the beam on the furthest part she could reach, the ladder creaking in protest from the precarious angle.

'That will have to do,' she sighed, climbing down to the safety of the dusty ground.

'No! That side is too droopy!'

Emily draped herself over the ladder in exasperation halfway down her descent, her head leaning against the surprisingly satisfying cold metal.

In the three months she had known Sarah she had quickly grown to love her brashness and even her sheer bossiness. Despite it all, she had a heart of gold and Emily found herself entrusting a lot in her. A good job too seeing as Sarah would one day be her sister-in-law. Emily's heart practically soared at the thought.

A quick admiring glance at her perfectly understated engagement ring made her smile as she checked the time on her wristwatch.

'It's dinner time, Sarah. Let's sort out droopy decorations afterwards.' Emily's tummy rumbled expectantly, having grown accustomed to the exact timing of the day in which it would be filled to the brim with Karen's delicious home cooking. She'd half expected to be the size of a house by now with all this indulgence, but the never-ending labouring work around the farm ensured Karen's food as a necessary energy source. It was safe to say that she had never been so satisfyingly exhausted and happy in her life.

Sarah and Emily abandoned their decorating for the time being, shutting the barn door behind them to shelter everything from the bitter winds. For almost a week now, Emily had been convinced of snow, but her new adopted Cornish family ensured her that, though it be cold, there was never a chance in hell of a white Christmas in Cornwall. They would just have to see.

It was a clear night, and the sky was the inkiest of blacks. The main farmhouse was a welcoming sight, as it always was after a long cold day on the farm, its windows glowing like a beacon in the darkness. An even more welcoming sight: a large figure in the shape of Emily's fiancé stood in the porchway, his hands hooked onto his hips as he watched the two ladies cross the large yard.

'I was seconds away from dragging you two out of that barn,' Tom's deep voice boomed into the quiet night. Emily gladly allowed herself to be enveloped into Tom's warm embrace, the delicious scent of Karen's cooking escaping out of the open front door.

'Alright, move you two. I'm starving,' Sarah grumbled, pushing herself past towards the direction of the kitchen.

'How's it all going?' Tom asked, his voice a gentle mumble as he looked down at Emily, her chin resting on his chest. 'My sister driven you insane yet?'

She smiled coyly. 'She's fine. But we might need your help after dinner to fix the main garland. I couldn't reach far enough.'

'Well of course you couldn't!' Tom scoffed. 'I like how she sent *you* up the bleddy ladder when she's about a foot taller than you!'

Emily felt her brow crease in gentle worry though her mouth twitched in amusement. This was Tom and Sarah's usual tendencies to totally wind each other up, and Emily had noticed recently that she seemed to be the centre of these sibling antics. Tom smoothed the flesh

7

between her brow with his thumb before planting a little kiss over the top.

'I'll sort it. Let's get some food first.'

The warmth of Karen's kitchen hugged Emily immediately and squelched any lingering cold in her limbs. For good measure, she made her usual beeline to the AGA and pressed her rear end against the heat. The rich smell of beef and red wine casserole filled the room as Karen dished up her usual generous portions for everybody. A thick slab of homemade pie pastry was placed haphazardly on each portion which Sarah passed along the table.

'Sit, sit!' Karen cried, swatting Emily gently with her tea towel as she curved around her to retrieve the cauliflower and cheese dish from the bottom oven. Emily smiled, the familiar bustle of dinner time in Karen's kitchen her absolute highlight of each day. She did as she was told and took her place by Tom at the large table, accepting a large glass of red from Steve.

'How many trees did you sell today, boys?' Karen asked Tom and Steve as she finally took her own place at the head of the table, in between Emily and Sarah. 'You looked busy when I drove in earlier from food shopping.'

'Ransacked, we were!' Steve said joyfully. 'All the reserved trees have been collected now. But lots more came in for ready-cut ones. You'd think everyone had their trees by now!'

'Well, traditionally people used to put their decorations up a fortnight to a week before Christmas Day,' Karen informed, still feeling the need to dish up vegetables from the centre table.

'That's boring!' Sarah piped up through a large mouthful of mashed potato. 'First of December – bam! - it's Christmas time as far as I'm aware!'

'Yes, we know,' Tom grumbled. Emily hid her amusement behind her wine glass as she took a sip of malbec. She knew exactly what he was referring to, having witnessed the festive frenzy which came over Sarah on the last few days of November, an explosion of decorations being set free from the attic on the first December morning. By lunchtime that same day, Sarah had had the whole family involved in transforming the main farmhouse and the barn conversions into Christmas grottos, even if they hadn't wanted to.

'Dad had always liked the decorations up early, you'll remember,' Sarah said, a little indignant. Steve squeezed his wife's shoulder, his silent way of keeping her temper down and showing her his support, no matter the topic.

'Yes, you're right there my love,' Karen chuckled. 'Before we'd started growing trees right here on the farm, your father used to be the first customer down to Tolcarne Farm in October to tag his choice.'

'October?' Emily cried, incredulous.

'We would have barely carved the pumpkins for Halloween before he was straight down there. Said the good ones will have already been reserved.'

'That's where Sarah got her nuttiness from,' Tom muttered, smiling wryly as he chewed, dodging a flying carrot slice from Sarah's direction. 'We had plenty of them queuing to reserve their trees straight after Halloween, I can assure you.'

'What about you, Em?' Steve piped up. 'When would you have usually put decorations up?'

Emily's smile quickly slipped from her face, all eyes on her. How to put it, without totally bringing down the mood. Because the truth was, she never had decorations to put up in that dingy old flat above the diner. She couldn't afford them. Gwynne's Diner downstairs had always had a pitiful little fake tree on the counter, with red and green paperchains hanging from the window – but that was about it. Besides, the rest of New York City, not to mention the office in Blake & Co, more than made up for it.

'Oh… well… not as early as you guys, that's for sure,' she said, chuckling nervously. 'Gwynne's Diner was right in the heart of a pretty big Jewish community anyway, so…' Emily's voice trailed off and her eyes diverted down to her plate. Yep, she was pretty sure she'd brought down the mood.

'I'm sure you had plenty of the New York festive glamour on your commute to work anyway, eh Em?' Steve said with encouragement.

She smiled in relief, thankful for Steve's easy nature. 'Exactly.'

'Just to annoy you all, I'm going to start a Halloween tree tradition next year,' Sarah blurted. Thank God for Steve's way with words and Sarah's inability to pick up on an awkward moment, bulldozing right through it with her own motivations.

Ten Days Until Christmas...

The tearoom had barely been open for an hour the next morning before a large batch line of hot chocolates were heading out to customers at different stages of their Christmas shopping rush. The coffee counter was a warzone of cinnamon powder, edible glitter and crushed gingerbread biscuits, as Emily topped yet another festive hot chocolate. Despite warnings to her ambitious business partner, Sarah had insisted on giving their customers not just two options for their hot chocolate menu – traditional and festive – but eight! And even then, the customers went rogue, putting in strange requests. Pinterest had been Emily's greatest friend recently for inspiration.

'Emily, a lady over on table five just asked whether you have any spaces left for the gingerbread house workshop next week,' Poppy said, ripping the next order from her pad and placing it on the cocoa dusted counter. 'Also, her After Eight hot chocolate was delicious, and she'd like another.'

'No problem. Pretty sure we've got two spaces left. I'll just check the diary.' Emily wiped her hands on a nearby cloth and grabbed the diary from under the till, still managing to leave glittery fingerprints on the white pages. 'Yeah, that's fine. Can you get her full name, phone number and a ten-dollar deposit?'

'Pound,' Poppy corrected, kindly. 'Ten-pound deposit.'

'Yes, sorry,' Emily chuckled. 'You'd think I'd get used to the currency by now. I'll make her drink now.'

Poppy took the diary over to table five just as Sarah skidded through the door from the kitchen, her

11

phone clenched in one of two fists currently being held above her head in animated excitement.

'Em, Em, Em! Guess what!'

'Mark's actually coming home for Christmas?' Steve repeated Sarah's words later that afternoon, after she'd announced it to the rest of the family at closing time in the tearoom. 'Like, actually spending Christmas Day here?'

'Don't sound so surprised,' Sarah bristled. She was adding yet another layer of decorations to the Nordmann Fir, leaving Emily and Poppy to sweep and clean the aftermath of over fifty hot chocolates for the day. 'Things have changed a lot since the wedding. Haven't they Tom?'

Tom was crouched in front of the wood burner, cleaning out the cold ash and prepping the fresh wood for next day's trade. He shrugged, impartial it seemed. 'I guess. Think I've spoken to him twice since the wedding, and that was mostly around the arrangements of Emily's move. Surprised he wants to give up his flash Christmas parties for a quiet roast in the countryside.'

'Oh, for God's sake! Mum?'

Karen was nursing a cup of tea, a worried expression playing on her gentle features. 'Hmm? Oh, I'm delighted my love. Of course!'

'What's the matter then?' Sarah cried, almost knocking the entire tree over with her gesticulations.

'I shipped all his presents last week. He won't have anything to open here!' The sheer concern and upset on her face made Emily want to wrap her future mother-in-law up in a huge hug. She really was the most caring person in the world.

'They may have arrived in the states by now,' Emily said, checking the calendar on her cell. 'Sarah, when is Mark flying over?'

'In the next couple of days, I think.'

'Text him and ask if he's received the presents yet, and he can bring some of the smaller ones back with him.'

12

'I'll do it now.' Sarah pulled her phone out from her back pocket and thudded out a quick message to her brother. Emily's eyes panned the room, checking where else needed a clean down, and she caught a glance of Tom's expression. Almost as much of a confusing mix as were some of the hot chocolate concoctions made on request this afternoon, Tom's features were hard to read as it seemed multiple emotions ran through him at once.

'Everything OK, there?' she asked Tom later, when they were alone and making their way to their little front door to freshen up before dinner. Emily still couldn't quite believe that Tom's little barn conversion had so quickly become *their* little barn conversion. Her own front door, complete with a handmade wreath which she'd made with Karen as a practise round for the upcoming wreath-making workshops they were advertising.

'I'm OK,' Tom said, feigning confusion in her question though it was clear that they both knew exactly what she was getting at. 'You OK?'

Emily ignored his attempt to make it about her and pressed on. 'Are you worried about Mark coming home?'

There was that shrug again. She'd quickly picked up on Tom's habit to shrug when he was uncomfortable or couldn't quite find the words.

'Things between us were never going to be perfect straight away,' Tom explained, an apology in his voice. He dug into his back pocket to retrieve his keys and unlocked the front door, stepping aside to let Emily into the warmth of their humble abode first. Tom made a beeline to the wood burner, stoking the old embers and preparing to relight it for the evening, as Emily headed behind the kitchen counter to make herself a cold drink. She stole little glances in Tom's direction; though she couldn't read his facial expression, the tension in his large shoulders said it all.

'What is actually worrying you? About Mark's return?' she asked gently from behind the counter. 'It is only for Christmas. He's not moving in.'

Tom's shoulders rose a few inches before falling heavily from a deep sigh. He heaved himself up from the wood burner, crossed the room towards her and placed a gentle kiss on her lips, his hand running through her bedraggled hair. She really needed to shower off the day.

'I'm OK,' he finally said. 'I'm sure it will be fine, and it will be nice for Mum to have all three of her children at home for Christmas, for once. Old habits die hard.'

Emily frowned up at him, a tinge of annoyance in her expression, but chose to give him the benefit of the doubt, announcing that she was heading upstairs for that much-needed shower.

She had just reached the middle of the spiral staircase leading upstairs as Tom added, 'just don't go running off with him back to New York.'

And there it was, the truth behind his concern, feebly disguised in a humorous tone. Except he clearly wasn't joking. Emily was about to retaliate when the front door closed gently shut and the sound of Tom's voice echoed in the cold yard outside as he took a phone call. That was the end of that discussion for a moment then. Emily vowed quietly to herself to not let him off too easily for that throw away comment as the calling of her shower won over, the urge to get rid of that sticky sweet mixed with roasted coffee smell which had embedded itself into every fibre of her hair.

Emily understood Tom's knee jerk protectiveness, and of course she knew *why* he had such trust issues with his brother. How could she forget what Mark had done to Tom all those years ago? Tom was right, things weren't going to be perfect or necessarily resolved between them just like that. But did he honestly believe that Emily would run back to New York with Mark?

Mark?! Really? When she had everything she could ever think to desire right here on this beautiful farm she now called home? She'd have to set things straight with Tom later, settle his concerns and remind him how happy she was here, with him. But she couldn't deny that she was a little miffed over his lack of faith in her. After all, *she* wasn't the one who broke his heart and her wedding vows all those years ago.

Nine Days Until Christmas...

There was a sort of giddy jig to Emily's steps this morning, as she followed Karen out into the gardens with a wicker basket on her arm, a pair of thick gardening gloves and secateurs in her opposite hand. They were on a scavenger hunt around the farm to pick the most festive-looking foliage they could for the wreath-making course that afternoon. Sarah was back at the tearoom with Poppy, making the final batch of mince pies for the workshop. Thankfully, they were much quieter today in walk-ins, with much less of a hot chocolate emporium going on behind the coffee counter.

'All right, what do we need to get, Karen?' Emily asked, donning the gloves, and giving her secateurs a determined chop-chop through the air.

'Lots and lots of eucalyptus. There's a great load of it over there,' Karen pointed to a straggly looking tree by the hedgerow. 'The tree itself isn't looking too great, but there's still plenty of good foliage left around the back of it if you don't mind clambering into the hedge. I think I saw some Old Man's Beard along the same hedge too. It's a type of clematis. You won't miss it.'

'I'm on it.'

'I'll see if there are any heads left on the hydrangeas over there,' Karen called as they headed in opposite directions. 'I've dried some back in the farmhouse but could do with more.'

As Karen had rightfully predicted, Emily had to literally clamber into the hedgerow, stomping down the prickly brambles with her boots to find a solid place in the stone and earth, to hoist her full weight. She gripped the trunk of the tree with her gloved hands and reached up to retrieve a large chunk of foliage, snipping away and chucking it next to her basket on the ground below. As she cut through and removed a particularly large piece of foliage, it cleared the view for her down the valley to The Old Riding School, which had apparently closed earlier in the year after the elderly owner had passed away. It had been emptied for months, but now it was very much bursting with life again, several moving vans crammed into the yard and the sound of drilling echoing across the fields. Emily made a mental note to mention it to everyone later.

It didn't take long to make a decent pile and she was soon clambering back down again, equal in her inelegance with her descend as she had been in her ascend. Just as she thought she had made it down in one piece, she felt her left foot tug against a pesky bramble. Her arms flailing uselessly, Emily had just enough time to discard the secateurs far away from her to at least avoid any form of impalement, before landing in a messy heap on the cold, wet grass below.

'Emily, my love! Are you alright?' Karen hollered from her side of the large gardens, picking up her pace to help Emily off the ground. 'Are you hurt?'

'Only my pride,' Emily chuckled, allowing Karen to pull her up. 'Have you noticed that there's people moving into The Old Riding School down there? Ooh, ouch! My ankle.'

'Careful, careful! Take my arm for support," Karen tutted, steadying Emily as she found her balance. 'Oh yes, look at that. Didn't know the place had come and gone on the market already. Fiona's children clearly didn't hang around in banking their inheritance from that place. Come on, let's get you into the warm. I'll send one of the boys back for the foliage.'

It was a slow struggle back to the tearoom, the closest of all the buildings with heating. Karen was surprisingly strong for someone in her 70s but, even with

Emily's slight frame, they were both panting by the time they got there.

'Foliage harvesting going well then,' Sarah scoffed, pulling out a chair next to the roaring wood burner for Emily to plonk herself down. 'What did you do? Fall into a rabbit hole?'

'Bramble entanglement,' Emily huffed, her ankle now twice its size and throbbing in large painful pulses. There were no customers at present, so she took the opportunity to hoist her leg up onto a spare chair as Poppy rushed over with a warm cup of coffee.

'Thanks, Poppy.' Emily smiled up at her in gratitude as Tom thundered through the tearoom door, closely followed by Steve.

'What happened?' Tom demanded.

'I've just twisted my ankle slightly on a bramble. Don't panic!'

'Saw you and Mum hobbling across the yard and thought it was your head!' Tom fussed, kneeling to examine her foot. Though it had been almost a month since her last cluster headache, Tom was still on high alert it seemed. 'What were you doing?'

'Collecting some eucalyptus for the workshop. Which, by the way, starts in only a few hours. Stop fussing please and get me some ice.'

'Already on it!' Sarah announced, coming through from the kitchen with a bag of ice wrapped in a tea towel.

'There's new owners moving into Fiona's old place,' Karen announced to the room as Sarah tended to Emily's ankle with the bag of ice.

'The Old Riding School?' Tom asked, grabbing a chair next to Emily and taking a seat. 'Didn't know it was for sale.'

'No, neither did I,' Karen admitted, then tutted. 'That's the market at the moment, unfortunately. Probably got snapped up by somebody up country before us locals even got a look in.'

'Fancied yourself a riding school, did you Mother?' Tom sniggered.

'Don't be cheeky.'

'It's looking pretty swollen, Em,' Sarah cut in, still tending to the ankle. 'Maybe you should get it looked at.'

'I agree,' Tom huffed, standing up and crossing his arms in protest. 'Come on, get in the car. I'll take you A&E.'

'You guys forget that I don't yet have the privilege of the NHS. It'll cost hundreds of pounds in health surcharge for them to tell me it's just bruised or something. Just give me an hour with this icepack and this delicious cup of coffee, and then I'll go right ahead with the workshop preparations.'

Emily stared them all down, one by one, with steely determination. Sarah shrugged and returned to the kitchen; Karen nodded with understanding and patted Emily's raised knee with affection before returning to the gardens to retrieve the cut foliage. Steve followed closely behind, offering his services to finish the job, whilst Tom remained in his towering position, his arms still crossed.

'I'm fine,' Emily smiled with assurance. 'You don't have to stay with me if you have lots to do.'

'It won't be a trigger for your head, will it?'

'My ankle? I shouldn't think so. Tom, please stop fussing. I fell out of a hedge. Hardly a major incident.'

'Your condition has been... behaving itself for a good month now. I'm just waiting for something to trigger it.'

'I've been in and out of remission before. A silly sprain won't trigger it, trust me.'

Tom's frown didn't falter but his arms relaxed from across his chest as he finally relented. 'I'll check on you in an hour. Make Sarah lead the workshop this afternoon. The cold will do it no good!'

Within only half an hour though, Emily's need to ensure this workshop was perfect for their guests got the better of her, and she was soon hobbling to the barn to set up the tables with their mossed wreath rings, reel wire and secateurs – a set for each station. Wooden apple crates from Tom's distillery sat in the middle of each table; she would fill those with a variety of the different foliage once Karen and Steve had brought them all down. There was a firepit in the middle of the shoehorn of workshop tables, ready to be lit closer to the time to keep their guests warm, and of course a demonstration table for Emily and Sarah. Then there a refreshments table for the mulled wine and minced pies in the far corner. Looking around at their handy work, she had to admit that the barn had been transformed into what she could only describe as a rustic winter wonderland. The garland, now without the droopiness, hung spectacularly above their demonstration table, showcasing all the foliage that their guests would be able to work with for their wreaths. A 10ft Nordmann Fir twinkled proudly near the entrance, surrounded by some of the pumpkins and squashes that were still going strong from their harvest festival.

Between them, Sarah and Emily had slowly worn Tom down with hosting more events on the farm, despite his best efforts to not let that happen. He'd been dubious about having 'public intrusion' on his farm more than ever, but even he had to admit that it had brought much needed revenue into the business, for both the cider farm and the tearoom. Business wasn't quite blooming yet, but it was certainly getting more and more popular. Emily was certain that their plans for the next wedding season in the New Year would make the big difference.

With just an hour to go before the workshop, Emily limped back to her little home (that would never get old) to check her appearance in the bathroom mirror and freshen up. She changed out of her wet, muddy clothes, and into some practical jeans and an old tee-shirt of Sarah's. Her hair was beyond help, falling limp and frizzy from the mizzle and damp that seemed to hang in the air on a permanent basis. Despite that, her mousy thin locks had still taken on quite the transformation since moving to the Cornish countryside. With the nutrition of Karen's cooking, and the fact she was ninety percent less stressed and near the brink of some sort of breakdown, her hair had grown and thickened an extraordinary amount in three months. She pulled it all back into a ponytail and assessed her final look. Well, she wasn't going to win prizes for glamour or fashion, but she was ready and practical for a wreath-making workshop with fifteen women in a cold barn in the middle of the countryside; and she was happy. Oh, so happy.

Out in the yard, a number of things happened at once.

Tom stomped his way across the muddy yard from the distillery, his finger wagging in Emily's direction. 'You should be taking your weight off that ankle, missus!'

Sarah came from the tearoom, her phone in her hand, looking somewhat bristled. 'One of the workshop women for tonight is messaging me *now* to tell me she's coeliac, and can I make her gluten-free mince pies? Really? Half an hour before the workshop?'

Karen and Steve made their way out of the barn, both soaking wet from their final trip to the fields.

'Emily my love, I've separated all the foliage evenly across the crates. Should be a lovely variety!'

Two vehicles crawled up the bumpy track and into the driveway: a shiny black Mercedes-Benz and a contrasting white Porsche. Both looked entirely out of place, and then the drivers stepped out.

'Merry Christmas!' Mark's voice boomed across the still yard, his headlights flooding the darkening farm. 'I know I'm early, but it was the last available flight with 1st class tickets. No way am I riding coach so close to Christmas!'

When no one moved, Mark eyed them up with concern and followed their line of sight to the other driver now stepping out of the Porsche, her long legs unfolding first before revealing her expensive cashmere coat and her platinum blonde curls.

'What the f...?' Sarah cursed. But Emily didn't hear the rest. Her blood was pumping loudly through her ears and her heart thudding painfully in her chest. She looked at Tom, his eyes glazed over in frightening rage, his jaw set in stone and his fists clenched tightly at his sides.

'Catherine?' Mark's voice was a strangle and he glanced at his family as realisation dawned on him at their reaction. His hands shot up in the air, palms facing out. 'She is *not* with me, I swear!'

Eight Days Until Christmas...

Mark should have known that his return home would trigger some sort of upset, but he never would have banked on it happening so quickly. With his bags in the boot and a briefcase bursting with paperwork from the office, which he'd brought with him to work on a client's campaign over the holiday, Mark had thought it would be nice to surprise his family with his first festive appearance in over four years.

Of course, he could fully rely on Catherine to ruin that.

The tension of last night's dealings sat heavy over breakfast the next morning and those gathered around Karen's kitchen table marvelled in suspicion over Catherine's appearance last night. Much to Sarah and Emily's horror, it came into fruition that Catherine had arrived to attend as one of the guests to the wreath-making workshop. Catherine! Tom's ex-wife. Mark's ex-lover. *The* Catherine who had almost permanently destroyed any hopes of a relationship between the two brothers. The Catherine that Mark foolishly fell in love with, who ran away to America with Mark, then left him hanging at the first opportunity for an upgrade! What was she even doing here on this side of the Atlantic Ocean? What was she doing, setting foot on Tregrouse Cider Farm again, after all these years? The stream of questions echoed around the kitchen.

'What's her angle?' Sarah spat through a mouthful of scrambled eggs, her fork stabbing into the air between them all menacingly. 'There's always a motive with that one! She did *not* just come to make pretty wreaths and consume festive refreshments! She's up to something – the little witch!'

'And that was extremely mild for you, my love,' Karen patted Sarah's hand from across the table. 'I thought you and Emily handled her remarkably last night.'

'I was ready to tell her to piss off!' Sarah admitted. 'But she'd be the type to make a scene and ruin our reputation. She was meeting four of the other ladies there.'

Sarah *had* certainly been on her best behaviour last night and even Mark had been beyond impressed with his fiery sister's reserved behaviour around the woman who had caused so much hurt in the family. In fact, Mark was almost disappointed that Sarah hadn't released her full fury on her, and rugby tackled her straight into the nearest puddle.

'How's Tom doing, my love?' Karen asked, turning to Emily. Mark practically squirmed in his seat at the sight of his mother looking so concerned, old guilt resurfacing from a past he'd put behind him.

'He's OK,' Emily smiled, though her efforts were feeble. 'You know Tom. He'll come round but he just needs some time to think.'

It was a bit of a euphemism to say the least. Mark had instantly recognised the darkness in Tom's eyes and the way he shut down. In fact, Tom hadn't so much as acknowledged Mark's arrival. So much for moving forward.

'Maybe I should just fly back to the states and leave it for this year,' Mark muttered, not meaning to sound so sultry.

An eruption of indignant protests came from Karen and Sarah as Steve did his upmost to set his facial expressions to something other than 'yeah, that probably isn't a bad idea.'

'Don't you dare, Mark!' Sarah barked, the fork-stabbing making a return. 'Don't be a coward and do a runner. I've got a feeling she'll be back, so you need to be here to support Tom. Eurgh…' All eyes darted to Sarah as she held her stomach, her fork poised in mid-air.

'Alright?' Steve asked, looking bewildered and leaning away from his wife.

'Thought I was going to be sick then. That's what the woman does to me. She makes me sick.'

Karen tutted. 'Well, is it any wonder the way you shovel down food? Dear life!'

Everyone returned to their meals as Sarah recovered and continued to devour her scrambled eggs, despite her mother's comment.

'You really think she'll be back?' Emily asked, her voice small. Mark observed her with sympathy as she pushed her food around the plate, her appetite fading away it seemed. Mark knew all too well Emily's fragile confidence, and a presence like Catherine was enough to bruise it entirely.

'Most definitely,' Sarah confirmed, clearly not picking up on the worry in Emily's voice. 'And if she's not here to spend money on the farm, I can't guarantee I plough her into a muddy puddle.' Mark snorted into his coffee, remembering his own devilish thoughts.

Sarah's expression softened and she seemed to go into a little fantasy of cashmere destruction. 'All that lovely white cashmere she was wearing last night.'

Emily found Tom in his office later that morning, supposedly doing invoices but clearly just needing a quiet place to stew. She hovered in the open doorway for a moment, contemplating leaving him to his thoughts, but her own insecurities got the better of her.

She tapped gently on the old wooden door frame, the green lead paint crackled and peeling away. 'Mind if I come in?'

Tom sat up and heaved a deep breath, like he'd been woken from a long trance. 'Of course not. You OK?'

Edging into the room, Emily was always surprised at how well the little stone building contained its heat, with the roaring fire in the corner creating warm shapes and shadows against the cold granite walls. When she reached Tom in his chair, she snaked her small arms around his broad shoulders and hugged him close from behind. 'Just worried about you.'

'I'm alright. Just came as a bit of a shock, is all.' His voice was low and sad. He squeezed her hand and rubbed her arm, his warmth radiating through her. She snuggled into his neck a bit more, taking in the familiar sweet, woody smell of his skin from hours in the distillery and the orchards. Tom's hands guided her around as he pulled her gently into his lap, enveloping her in and cocooning her in blissful heat. It really was freezing outside.

'Tom?'

Tom made a deep noise of acknowledgement.

'You know Mark had nothing to do with this right? Don't let her come between you any more than she already has.'

There was a pause and Emily felt Tom's body go rigid around her for a moment as he took in her words.

'No, I know,' he said finally. 'Give me the day to clear my head a bit. I'll be there at dinner time to greet him properly. How's that?'

'Super.' Emily smiled. That's all she could ask at this moment. She kissed him gently and ran her hand down the side of his stubbly face before reluctantly getting up and leaving him in peace.

Back outside in the yard, the easterly chill cut through her multiple layers, the absence of Tom's warmth making the drop in temperature more prominent. She made a swift beeline to the tearoom, knowing that the tiny little stone building would be radiating in wood burner heat by now. She was right, and the delicious smell of festive spices coming from the kitchen were enough alone to warm her through.

'Oh my god, Sarah! What is that delicious smell?' Emily shouted towards the kitchen as she rounded the counter to make herself a warming coffee.

'Lebkuchen!' Sarah hollered back, sticking her head around the kitchen door to ask Emily to make her a coffee while she was at it.

'Leb-koo-chun?' Emily paused, looking at her in confusion.

'You know...? Those Christmas biscuits from Germany.'

'Leyb-koo-kuhn?' Emily corrected, though not doing much better justice to the German dialect.

'Yeah. That'll be the one,' Sarah said, distracted as the rest of her body appeared from around the doorway. She slid the plate of biscuits down the counter towards Emily. 'Think I've used way too much nutmeg! Try one.'

Emily bit into one in the shape of a snowflake. It was soft, with the slightest crunch from the chopped nuts Sarah had added, a definite note of nutmeg but, in her opinion, not overpowering. 'That's delicious Sarah. I don't think the nutmeg is too much at all.'

'Think I've sampled too many,' Sarah groaned, bringing a hand to her chest as she belched loudly. 'Feeling sick again.'

Emily glanced at Sarah with worry. Come to think of it, she did look a bit peaky. 'Are you coming down with something? You really shouldn't be around the food if you are.'

'No, I'm fine,' Sarah replied, indignant. 'I've just overindulged. Nothing new there. Hold off on that coffee, actually. I'll have a glass of water instead.'

'OK, now I know something is wrong. You're drinking water... voluntarily.'

Sarah shot Emily a deadpan expression before returning to the kitchen, still clutching her stomach. 'Eat your lebkuchen.'

Back in the main house, Mark was finding himself unusually distracted from his work. He'd promised his mother that he'd spend no more than a couple of hours on his laptop this morning completing his work, thinking it would be plenty of time to send out some emails and tie any loose ends ready to go on his well-earned holiday break. But right now, his mind was a fog of questions, and his body was practically trembling with the urge to seek Catherine out and demand answers.

Without Sarah's palpable anger to compensate, he realised he was bloody angry.

Beside his nerves, he'd been looking forward to coming home for Christmas. He'd actually been somewhat excited by the idea of spending some quality time with his sister and mum, rebuilding a relationship with his brother and having a good catch up with Emily. He'd even considered the idea of sharing a good whiskey with Steve. He was his brother-in-law now, after all.

Now, he had that all too familiar urge to jump on a plane and get away as fast as possible. For someone who could handle themselves in a business meeting, Mark was terrible with confrontation, and he knew all too well that Catherine's unexpected return to Cornwall, and the farm for that matter, could only bring up old hurt and conflict between him and his family. He was tired of the fight, tired of being on the outside. He might live and work three thousand miles across the Atlantic, but he was enjoying being a part of his family again.

'Still at it?' his mother's disapproving voice rang across the kitchen as she shuffled in, peeling off her wet anorak and draping it across the back of one of the dining chairs in front of the AGA. 'Dear, dear – that light mist seems to be enough to soak you right through. Tom and Steve are going to be drowned rats by the end of the day, selling trees in this weather.'

Mark knew, in truth, that nothing Karen ever said was a deliberate dig at him, but old habits die hard. Suddenly he felt that he should be closing his laptop down, donning some old clothes and getting out there in the miserable weather to help sell some of those damn trees.

'Just a bit distracted,' Mark mumbled into his hands. Despite the heat of the AGA, the usual harrowing breeze sliced through his thick jumper and his fingers were beginning to feel frozen and gnarled over his keyboard.

Karen had paused behind him, pondering, and Mark could feel her presence behind him. He was waiting for a barrage of comments about working on a screen for too long or something about just enjoying his time off – *it was Christmas after all*. He didn't quite expect what she said next, her hands patting either side of his shoulders in a matter-of-fact way. 'You know what they say, my love. Nothing left to do sometimes than to just face the music.'

Mark's face creased in confusion as he lifted his head from his hands and looked up. 'What?'

'Go and talk to your brother!' Karen cried in exasperation. 'If that little...so-and-so does come back to the farm, wouldn't it be better for you both to face her together? To let her know that your brotherly relationship is still going strong.'

'Oh yeah, strong as a paper bag,' Mark replied, ruefully.

'Get on with you! Go! Talk to your brother!' Karen proceeded to usher her son out of his chair. 'And while you're at it, shift some Christmas trees.'

He should have seen that one coming.

Seven Days Until Christmas...

'We finally have a night off from festive workshops, baking or book work,' Emily huffed, out of breath from exertion. 'And you're dragging me to the local pub to meet with your friend who hates me?'

Sarah and Emily were stumbling inelegantly down the dark road leading to the Smuggler's Inn, Emily's grumpy mumbles audible all the way down the muddy track. With all the cars parked alongside the hedges either side, it had been a squeeze for Tom's enormous 4x4, so he'd reluctantly dropped them off at the top of the hill nearest the village.

'Katie doesn't hate you,' Sarah reasoned, before changing tune. 'Actually, scrap that. She hates everybody! But don't take it personally. I still say you should have borrowed my heels. You're already about a foot shorter than me. I feel like a bloody giant next to you.'

'I can't walk in heels on a flat sidewalk in Manhattan. What makes you think I'll manage a bumpy track?'

'Fair point. You can blame Mother for this, partly. She's forcing the boys to have some sort of bonding time over cider and curry tonight. Steve is completely incensed by the whole thing. Bloody hell, it's busy.'

Sarah heard an audible groan escape from Emily. Fully aware how uncomfortable crowds made Emily by now, she linked arms with her sister-in-law-to-be and gave that arm an encouraging squeeze. 'Come on, Em. Let's keep you young and less boring.'

They stepped into the warmth of the old pub, the buzz of the place hitting them as they laughed together, finding Katie waving them down with little enthusiasm from a table in the corner by the bar.

Back at the farm, the silence in the room was palpable as Tom, Mark and Steve each took great interest in the cider bottles in their hands. It had been almost ten whole minutes since the last person had spoken.

'Label's wonky on this bottle, Tom mate,' Steve commented.

'Where?' Tom leaned forward, inspecting the bottle in Steve's hands. 'Oh, yeah.'

Another silence claimed the room as Tom proceeded to inspect his own bottles.

'Mine's wonky too,' Tom finally announced to the room. Mark cocked an eyebrow, watching with indifference as the two got up to check the ones in the fridge.

'So, she just rocked up? At the farm? No explanation?' Katie blurted out, as Sarah finished telling her friend about Catherine's sudden appearance at the farm.

'Yep. She's up to something. She did not travel back from the states and rock up to her ex-husband's farm to do a wreath-making workshop. Oh, sorry Em,' Sarah said, noticing the flinch cross Emily's face. 'We can drop the topic if you like.'

'It's OK,' Emily said, smiling sweetly and waving her off. She was clearly far from OK. 'It's just hearing Tom being referred to as her ex-husband.'

'Didn't she know they were married?' Katie barked at Sarah, pointing at Emily.

'No, I did... it's just hearing it out loud. It's just...icky.'

Katie cocked an eyebrow. 'Icky. Did she seriously just say icky?'

Sarah watched Emily retreat a little bit more and her heart went out to her. This was difficult enough for the

31

family, but Sarah couldn't imagine how uncomfortable Emily must be feeling about Catherine's mystery return to the farm.

'I don't get it,' Katie went on, her elbows propped on the sticky table and her drink sloshing around menacingly. 'Is she here to get Tom back?'

'God, I hope not,' Emily said, looking horrified.

'Even if she is, is Tom likely to go back to her?'

'Definitely not,' Sarah confirmed, patting Emily on the hand reassuringly. 'Think he'd rather scoop his eyes out with a rusty spoon!'

'So, why are you moping?' Katie snapped, officially spilling her drink. 'Tom is with you! You're engaged and he's bleddy smitten with you... for some reason...'

'Oh, thank god for that last part,' Sarah snided. 'I was beginning to think you were becoming compassionate. Ow!' She rubbed her arm, having received a playful punch from her friend. *Wham!*'s Last Christmas began to play from the pub's jukebox and Sarah thought for a moment how apt some of the lyrics were.

'No, Katie is right,' Emily finally said. 'I need to stop worrying about something that hasn't, and hopefully isn't, going to happen.' Then, sitting up straight and determined, 'I have no reason to be threatened by this woman.'

'Ere! Sarah, my love,' Patty whispered, scuttling over and sandwiching herself in next to a bemused Katie. Her and her husband owned the Inn, and she was the first one to stick her nose in people's business. 'Don't go telling me that's Tom's bleddy ex-missus over there! Bleddy hell, she's got some nerve, eh? You want me to ban her?'

Sarah followed Patty's line of vision over to the far side of the bar where Catherine was indeed propped elegantly on a stool, her infuriatingly perfect hair in infuriatingly perfect waves as she spoke to a person beside her, a wine glass poised in a well-manicured hand. She then looked at Emily and found that her previously determined stance not to be threatened had crumbled into pieces.

'OK, who am I kidding?' Emily groaned. 'She's like someone straight off run-way! Why is she here?'

Sarah and Emily jumped as Katie's fist thumped the table. 'That's it. This is ridiculous. I'm going over there.'

They watched in mild amusement as Katie crossed the pub floor in less than ten strides and approached Catherine with the kind of confidence only Katie possessed.

'See?' Sarah said to Emily as Patty scuttled off again. 'Hates everybody but fiercely loyal to those she tolerates enough to call friends.'

Katie's words travelled, even over the loud buzz of a busy evening. Catherine looked both bewildered and irritated to be interrogated in this way and suddenly her eyes darted over Katie's shoulders and landed directly on their table.

'Well, this is a nice coincidence,' Catherine said, her voice like caramel but her eyes narrowed. 'My wreath is hanging proudly on my door. Such a wonderful evening. Well done, you. Aren't you clever?'

Sarah gritted her teeth. To an external person, that had been a perfectly pleasant way to open up a conversation. But Sarah knew Catherine all too well, and her subtle tones of insincere sincerity didn't go unnoticed.

'Why are you back?' Sarah blurted out, suddenly not feeling the restraints of having to be polite this time now that Catherine was no longer a paying customer.

'Goodness me, I've lost count how many times I've been asked that today,' Catherine smiled sweetly. 'I forgot how nosy everybody around here was.'

Catherine's eyes settled on Emily and Sarah felt a rush of protectiveness for her future sister.

'It's a reasonable question,' Sarah continued, 'given how you left things.'

Catherine looked almost bored as Katie barged past her to take her seat again. 'Yes well, the past is the past. We all know how much you Trengrouses like to dwell in it.'

Sarah felt the anger towards Catherine bubble within and – what was that? – nausea? She'd never been literally sick with anger before. Catherine was lucky Sarah hadn't punched her lights out yet. She was surprised when Catherine's cool composure faltered for a moment, her arms dropping to her sides in a sort of defeat.

'Listen, I didn't intend to start any trouble or for us to compete in any sort of stand-off,' Catherine began. 'My business... my reasons for being here is personal. But I won't be here for long, you can count on that. You can all get back to your happy little family charade.'

Catherine's eyes burned into Emily's just that little bit longer and Sarah's sisterly protectiveness towards her almost got the better of her before she suddenly froze, her hand clutching her stomach once again.

'What are you doing?' Catherine demanded, taking a step back.

'Nothing... I'm just –'

Sarah's words were cut short as her body arched forward and the contents of her stomach was emptied all over the pub floor and Catherine's predictably expensive cream suede boots. Later, when her stomach wasn't retching horribly, Sarah would perhaps giggle in glee, but for now she had more pressing matters to consider. And she knew exactly how her husband was going to take it.

'Pregnant? Like – pregnant, pregnant?' Steve's voice had risen an octave above his norm, his eyes wild and wide. The evening had been drawn to an abrupt and slightly messy end, with a quick detour to the supermarket by taxi.

'I wasn't aware of more than one type of pregnant! Yes, pregnant bloody pregnant!'

'And you're absolutely sure?'

'Two ridiculously expensive piss sticks tell me so!'

'But how did that happen?'

'Really Steve, do I need to explain it to you?' Sarah hissed, closing her eyes as she leaned on the back of the

34

nearest chair. The waves of nausea seemed intensified now she knew the cause of it.

Steve's eyes glazed over for a moment before his face broke out in a wide grin. 'This is fantastic! Bleddy brilliant!'

Sarah's jaw almost hit the floor, along with her stomach. Perhaps she didn't know exactly how he'd react after all. 'It is?'

'Of course! Don't you think?'

'I'm not sure yet.' She grimaced, supressing a belch and taking a steady breath. 'Hard to get excited right now with my stomach doing occasional somersaults. Eurgh, I drank a lot of booze tonight, and I'm pregnant! I'm a terrible mother already!'

'Don't be daft! You didn't know and I'm sure one night of drinking won't do much harm.'

'Yeah... one night... '

Steve's arms enveloped his worried wife as she groaned into his chest. 'It will be fine. I'm so happy.'

'Yeah...' Sarah relented. 'Me too.'

Six Days Until Christmas...

It was an unusually clear, bright morning. The sun gleamed off the thin layer of frost blanketing the farm and there was a delicious aroma of festive spice in the air.

Emily darted around frantically, taking the gingerbread biscuits out of the oven and checking the progress of the stollen. Tonight was their gingerbread house workshop and, with Sarah fast asleep in bed after a night of being unwell, Emily was suddenly left to run the tearoom for the day. On top of that, there were the fifteen sets of gingerbread walls, roofs and chimney stacks to cut out and bake, not to mention run the actual workshop later on in the evening. She didn't like to admit to a guilty Sarah that she'd never built a gingerbread house in her life, let alone teach it. How did the famous saying go? Something about the blind leading the blind.

'Let me guess,' Tom's deep voice rumbled through the small building as he reached Emily in the little kitchen, now removing the fully baked stollen from the oven. 'Sarah and Katie tried to drink each other under the table last night and now she's hungover with her head down the toilet.'

Emily paused, as she pricked the stollen with a knitting needle to check it was full baked. Sarah hadn't specifically said not to tell Tom, but something told her she wouldn't be happy with Emily if she gave away her news to her eldest brother.

'Something like that,' Emily said, simply.

'Yeah… well,' Tom huffed, biting into a piece of gingerbread, 'she's taking the piss. Anything I can help with?'

'You can stop eating my chimney stacks, for one,' Emily scolded, batting his hand away before he could steal any more. 'I've got to make fifteen of these all together. Does it taste OK? Enough spice?'

'It's delicious,' Tom said, shooting her an apologetic look as he finished the rest of his piece. He rolled up his sleeves and started washing the dishes, much to Emily's gratitude. 'By the way, not to add to your stress – your arty farty friend from New York tried to video chat on Mum's iPad last night. She only noticed this morning.'

'Michelle? She must have forgotten the time difference. I'll try her back later.'

Mark was well aware, as he drove down the bumpy lane towards Fiona's old place, that this was a very bad idea. It was only a hunch, but he was pretty sure he knew who the new owner was. His hunch was proven correct as he pulled into the yard, right next to the white Porsche.

So, Catherine had bought herself a riding school. There was something he never thought he'd see.

The Old Riding School was just as he remembered it. There had been times in his childhood when he and Sarah had crossed the short distance through the orchards to get to Fiona's. On his father's orders, he and Sarah had come down here every Saturday afternoon to help the elderly lady clean out the stables and brush down the horses. In exchange, they'd get a free hack and a piece of cake on their return.

Karen had informed him of Fiona's passing over six months ago, and he'd been extremely sad of the news. Being back here now, with some of those fond memories trickling back in, he suddenly felt quite heavy hearted.

Already, in the short time that the farm had changed hands, there was a drastic change. The stables were clearly half-way through some sort of transformation, with some of them donning new double-glazed doors and windows, whilst the rest were empty shells full of building materials. The main cottage itself was currently dressed to the very top in scaffolding, and several large skips sat full to the brim in the main yard. The sound of delicate footsteps distracted him from his exploration, and he closed his car door with a soft thud.

'Mark?' Catherine leaned over her garden gate, her platinum blonde curls spilling over and framing her face. 'To what do I owe this pleasure?'

It was a fair question. Now he was here, Mark wasn't so sure himself. 'I don't mean to be blunt, Catherine. But what the hell are you doing here?'

Catherine shrugged. 'Buying a riding school. Clearly.'

'You hate horses.'

She smiled, amused by the conversation. But Mark noted that edge to her expression which often gave away a deep irritation.

'Was that everything?' Catherine asked. 'Only, I'm very busy.'

'So, you've just abandoned your glamourous life in sunny California to live on an old muddy equestrian centre in the middle of nowhere? Can't say I'm buying it.'

'Does it really have any impact on you?' There was the irritation, now fully surfacing across her harsh features. 'It's not really any of your business now, is it?'

'No impact on me, no. Kind of my business, though,' Mark rebutted, using his coolest voice, often saved for those tricky clients back in the office, his hands in his pockets in a nonchalant way. 'I'm sure, with your sort of budget, you could have had any muddy old patch of land in Cornwall. But of course, you choose to live next door to the cider farm. What are you trying to do? Torture them?'

'Of course not! Why would you even think that?' she snapped. Mark shrugged in response, and she huffed, folding her arms across her chest. 'Real nice, Mark. Can you just go, please? I really am very busy.'

Catherine glanced in the direction of the cottage behind her, perhaps for the third time, and Mark realised then that she looked uncomfortable. Nervous, even.

'OK,' Mark agreed, holding his palms face out in front of him. 'Sorry to disturb you. Just... leave Tom to live in peace, will you?'

Before Catherine had a chance to answer back, or so much as glare in his direction, a small woman came out of the cottage and made her way slowly towards Catherine, calling her name in confusion.

'Cathy? Who's your friend?' the woman said, cheerfully. She wore a Christmas tree hat and her jumper flashed merrily in festive reds and greens.

'Grace, I told you to stay inside.' It was far from a reprimanding tone. In fact, Mark was momentarily shocked in the gentleness of Catherine's voice. He watched as she relented and placed a protective arm around the woman's shoulders, despite her clearly being Catherine's senior. 'This is Grace. My sister.'

'Older sister, I'd like to add,' the woman said cheerfully. She had the most infectious smile that even Mark found himself returning the gesture. 'Just because I'm about a foot shorter than you, doesn't mean I'm not in charge.'

'Oh, you're definitely in charge,' Catherine smiled. It was a side of her Mark had never seen before, and it certainly softened her features considerably.

Mark blushed a little as Grace caught him looking a little longer than was necessary. She shrugged, with a good-natured smile. 'It's only an extra chromosome.'

'I wasn't...' Mark began but was shameful at being caught staring. The truth was, he'd been drawn to the way Grace radiated with happiness, bringing the very best out of even someone like Catherine. He'd literally only captured a few seconds of their relationship and he found it quite remarkable.

'Grace, would you mind excusing us for a moment. I'll be back with you just as soon as I've said goodbye to Mark.'

'See ya!' Grace waved cheerfully at Mark, which he returned. When she was safely out of ear shot, back in the cottage, Mark turned his attention back to Catherine.

'You have a sister?'

'So it seems,' Catherine drawled. When Mark shot her a look of impatience, she added, 'I've only known this myself for about a year.'

A silence fell between them. Mark couldn't begin to find an appropriate response. There was a rare vulnerability to Catherine which disarmed Mark, his intention to confront her fizzling away completely.

'You can reassure your lot that I'm not moving in,' Catherine snapped. 'I'm merely here to settle Grace in and oversee the conversion. I'm not here to cause trouble. You're flattering yourselves if you think my short return has anything to do with you Trengrouses.'

There was that Catherine aggression that Mark knew all too well, but he suddenly realised that this aggression was just a front to protect a much more vulnerable side.

'A conversion, you say?' Mark probed, attempting to diffuse her temper.

'A retreat. For the disabled,' Catherine said bluntly, her arms crossed again. 'You may have noticed that Grace has Down's Syndrome. I think it's one of the reasons I've only recently found out about her. My parents didn't want her or something, which is bloody disgusting! She's actually very independent and self-sufficient, so there really was no excuse for their abandoning her.'

She spat these words out, showing that her anger was still very much fresh.

'Anyway, in the short time I've known Grace, she has talked non-stop about this retreat she once went on in the Cotswolds. Arts and crafts, horse riding – even spa. Just got me thinking...where better to retreat than in Cornish countryside?'

Mark scoffed. 'Wouldn't have heard you say that once upon a time.' Then, changing his tune, he said, 'it's a nice thing you're doing.'

'It's just a little leg up for Grace,' Catherine said. 'She'll be perfectly capable of running it, with the help of a small team.'

A heavy silence fell between them for a moment and Catherine sniffed impatiently, drumming her fingers on the wooden gate.

'We're having a little Christmas festival here on the twenty-third,' Catherine said, sounding bored. 'Doubling up as a soft-opening event. Um... spread the word... or come along if you want. Whatever.'

The twenty-third. Why did that date ring a bell for Mark?

'Oh no! You're sure? The twenty-third?' Emily gasped an hour later, after Mark had gone straight to find her on his return to the farm.

'Yeah. But it's more of a soft opening for her sister's retreat. I doubt it'll have any impact on your Winter Wonderland festival,' Mark said, trying to reassure Emily as she stressed over a bowl of icing.

'Really, Mark?' Emily said, dropping the spatula into the bowl and waving the poster around frantically. Grace had overheard Mark and Catherine talking about the festival and had run out of the cottage in excitement to give him a poster of the big event.

Emily straightened the paper and read from the events list. 'Christmas cookie decorating. Santa Claus and reindeers. Real-life ones, I'd like to add. Wreath-making workshops! Sarah knew she'd been up to something when she came to ours the other day. Oh, my god – Sarah is going to freak.'

'Look, I know this isn't ideal,' Mark reasoned, leaning against the door frame between the kitchen and the tearoom, which was brimming with customers after their hot chocolate fix. Poppy was seen flitting between tables and the counter, which had been subjected to another one of its cocoa powder explosions. 'Catherine is trying to do something nice... for her sister.'

Emily remarked him for a moment before putting the poster down and returning to her icing, which was in danger of setting.

'I didn't realise you two were still friendly.' Emily wasn't sure why this bothered her. Perhaps because of Tom – because of how much both Mark and Catherine had hurt him in the past. For them to suddenly be friends again seemed almost a complete kick in the face.

'We're not,' Mark replied, sternly. 'I actually went over there to tell her to back off. But her sister's sudden appearance changed things. I *am* on Tom's side, you know. I won't doing anything to tarnish things between us again.'

'OK,' Emily said, feeling bad as she cast an apologetic look in his direction. 'Sorry, I'm just really stressed. I overcooked the last batch of gingerbread for tonight's workshop, the tearoom has been busy from the moment we opened the doors, and I can't seem to get the right consistency with this god damn icing.' She threw the spatula back in the bowl and pushed it away, taking in a deep breath.

'Wow. Maybe you should have stayed with Blake&Co. Far less stressful.'

A tea towel was flung in his direction and they both chuckled for a moment, the tension easing momentarily.

'Seriously though,' Emily said, returning reluctantly to her bowl. 'We've been advertising our Winter Wonderland for over a month now. Sarah says it's become a bit of a Trengrouse tradition over the years.'

'I can confirm that, being a Trengrouse myself,' Mark added, wryly.

'But whether it's for her sister or not, it was a bit of a crappy thing to do. Turning up like that. Being all underhand and secretive about it. She knew exactly what she was doing.'

'Maybe,' Mark relented. 'Underhand is often Catherine's specialty. But, for once, I do think her motives were genuine. Actually, I had a little idea on the short drive home. We're going to need to speak to Tom, and my guess is that he won't be massively happy with the prospect.'

Five Days Until Christmas...

Emily woke with the smell of gingerbread practically embedded into her nostrils the very next morning. She wasn't sure she wanted to look at another gingerbread house ever again.

The workshop had been a success, with fifteen gingerbread houses leaving the tearoom mostly intact. One poor lady had a slight mishap towards the end of the workshop when she overloaded her roof with an assortment of gummies and icing. But there had been festive music, mulled wine, and laughter galore the entire evening, made much more enjoyable for Emily than the wreath workshop given that Catherine wasn't there to make her feel small and inferior. Instead, she'd felt mildly confident and competent as she'd circulated the room, overseeing the gingerbread construction, and offering a helping hand when things got a little tricky.

Sarah had surfaced mid-afternoon, but the strong festive aromas of the mulled wine and gingerbread had quickly turned her green again, so Emily had insisted she stay away. She was grateful to Mark and Tom for pitching in with the drink making and clearing up and was delighted to see Karen enjoying herself in the workshop with a friend from her WI group. As Tom had said to her last night as he took another tray of mulled wine and minced pies to the tables, it was nice to see Karen relax and be waited on for once.

Even though she'd showered last night before bed, Emily jumped in the shower again in hopes of stripping her senses of the sticky sweet smell. She had the morning off, courtesy of Sarah who had managed to get out of bed this morning with just a hint of nausea. The sun was out bright and strong, and the ground was hard from the frost, so Emily suddenly craved a walk with the dogs.

Emily's country attire had improved over the months since she'd permanently moved on to the farm. She'd exchanged the swamped, oversized trench coat she'd been commandeering for a much more flattering Barbour jacket, which Tom had recently treated her to. She stuffed some poop bags and her cell phone into the pockets of that same jacket, and away they were through the fields and towards the back lanes, the whippets barking and billowing in front.

As always, it didn't take long for Emily to reach the little kissing gates that led to the back lanes, that very spot always making her smile as she thought of the sheep fiasco back in September, literally being lifted to safety by Tom. It was something Tom had done ever since: making her feel safe.

Her usual route took a small detour, and she found herself beelining towards The Old Riding School, her curiosity getting the better of her. Mark had shared his big idea with her last night on how to allow Catherine's Christmas Festival to have the least impact on their Winter Wonderland. In theory, it was a good idea. But how Tom was going to react today when Mark ran it by him, she did not know.

The place was buzzing with movement of the construction kind, and it almost seemed like every builder and stone mason within a ten-mile radius was on site. The stables had been stripped back and were being converted into what looked like accommodation at an alarming rate. Emily caught sight of Catherine over on the far side of the yard, in deep conversation with a man with a clipboard and a hard hat, looking as infuriatingly glamourous as the last time Emily saw her. Even in her shiny new Barbour jacket, Emily suddenly felt scruffy. What was the expression Steve often used? Like she'd been dragged through a hedge backwards. Despite herself, Emily smiled at the expression.

She was beginning to get used to her new family's funny phrases and idiosyncrasies, and she even found herself adopting a few of them herself.

Deciding she'd probably lurked in the shadows like a creep long enough, Emily turned with the intention to head back towards the cider farm. The whippets had other plans however, as they both launched themselves over the stone stile and bolted towards an unexpecting cat trying to bathe in the December sun.

'Molly! Lula!' Emily hissed, hiding feebly behind some bracken. Panicking, she pretended to be particularly interested in the golds and browns of the dying old fern leaves. But the whippet duo had already given her away, and her heart almost plummeted as Catherine clocked her position and started making her way over. Before she could even think of an acceptable way of dealing with her current predicament, Emily found herself doing the one thing she probably shouldn't have done. The whippets barked in excitement and leapt the stile in one hurdle, chasing after Emily as she ran as fast as her welly boots would allow her.

'You ran away?' Mark said, laughing as he followed her into the tearoom an hour later. She'd returned the dogs to the main house, vowing in futility to never speak to them or so much as pat them ever again, and taken herself to the tearoom with her head hanging in shame. 'So, you literally hid in the bushes, spied on her and, when you got caught, ran away from her!'

'I wasn't planning on spying on her. I didn't spy on her!' Emily cried, hitting Mark with a tea towel as he continued to roar with laughter. 'I was walking by and noticed all the commotion with the renovation. The dogs chased down a poor cat in the yard. It was totally innocent.'

'Nothing innocent about legging it like that,' Mark pointed out, collapsing into a fresh wave of laughter.

'What's so hilarious?' Tom asked, ducking his head as he stooped into the kitchen area. He looked irritated and threw his brother a look which only brought back some not-so-distant memories of their feud. Emily frowned at him, only to receive a defensive shrug in return.

'Nothing,' Emily replied, with warning in her tone as she gave Mark a scolding look.

'Emily ran away from Catherine after spying on her at The Old Riding School.'

'Mark!'

'Riding school?' Tom asked, his irritation deepening.

'Yeah, Catherine bought Fiona's old place,' Mark said, now frowning. He turned on Emily. 'Didn't you tell him?'

'Not yet, no,' Emily said, suddenly uncomfortable with Tom's darkening expression. 'You were meant to talk to him about your idea.'

'Well, I just assumed you two do actually speak to each other and that you'd have covered the basics,' Mark sniped.

'Yes, well… clearly nobody here has bothered to fill me in,' Tom muttered, unamused. Then, as deep hurt flashed across his lovely features, he said, 'anything that involves *her*… I'm not sure I want to hear it. Especially from you, Mark. Excuse me.'

Emily gasped with guilt as Tom made a quick exit for the door, just as Mark huffed in defence.

'God dammit, Mark! You could not have been more insensitive!' Emily cried, barging past him and going after Tom, who was now half-way across the yard already. 'Tom! Wait a minute!'

Her shouts across the yard quietened to her normal volume when Tom finally paused and allowed her to catch up.

'Tom. Don't be angry. It wasn't as mysterious and secret as Mark made it sound. He went to see her and…'

'Catherine!' Tom rounded on Emily, the pain in his face palpable. 'It's Catherine, Em! You know the history... and Mark!' Tom's fists clenched either side of him as he battled with the rage and anguish coursing through his body. 'It's like he can't help himself!'

'Tom...'

'Why are you getting involved? With him? With *her?*'

'Tom, please. You've got this all wrong.'

Without warning, tears began to stream down Emily's face and a sense of panic took over. By default, this was the only way Emily knew how to face confrontation of any kind and she mentally kicked herself for allowing her past trauma to overshadow Tom's pain. Tom's anger faltered and fizzled into frustration, but he gathered her into him all the same, holding her tight, silently letting her know that she was safe, no matter what.

'We're OK,' Tom assured, stroking Emily's hair. 'But I can't be a part of anything involving *her*.'

'I know,' Emily mumbled, drawing in Tom's scent, and allowing it to calm her. 'But it doesn't involve *her* per se.'

Tom drew back, sighing heavily through his nostrils. 'Whatever it is, I can't. I'm sorry. I need to get back to selling trees. We're fine, don't go panicking that we're not. But please, just... respect my wishes.'

Before Emily could say any more, Tom squeezed her shoulder and strode purposefully across the rest of the yard, disappearing behind the distillery.

'It was awful, Sarah. He was so angry and hurt. I could have killed Mark!'

With the tearoom closed after another fruitful day, Emily was now mopping the floor, the chairs stacked up on all the tables and Sarah taking deep, steadying breaths over a glass of water. Emily had explained everything to Sarah, including the unfortunate clash with their Winter

48

Wonderland and Catherine's Christmas Festival. As for Mark's big idea, Sarah was somewhat quiet about that.

'He never was very tactful,' Sarah tutted, her elbow on the table as she rubbed her forehead cathartically, willing the increasing nausea to go.

'Are you OK?'

'It's like the hormones tripled as soon as the test confirmed I was pregnant!'

'Have you told your Mom yet?' Emily asked, raising an eyebrow. She knew Sarah had been avoiding it, but still struggled to understand why.

'I will! I will! I'm just waiting for the right time. She might think it's too soon. Or worse, she'll fuss over me and be unbearable!'

'Doesn't sound so bad,' Emily reasoned, thinking of how Karen's fussing and care for everyone around her was exactly why she loved it here. Thanks to Karen and this little family, she'd never felt so loved and cared for in her life.

Sarah groaned and sipped her water, rotating her hand impatiently. 'Keep me distracted! Keep reminding me why my brothers are complete donuts.'

'He won't even hear the plan,' Emily blurted out.

'Who?' Sarah said to the floor as her elbows migrated to her knees.

'Tom... keep up!' Emily scolded, and Sarah snorted in amusement. 'He said that he couldn't be a part of anything that involved *her*.'

Sarah looked up from her compromised position and arched an eyebrow in Emily's direction. 'Can you blame him?'

Emily sighed in defeat. 'No. No, I can't.'

Four Days Until Christmas...

Christmas, although a hopeful time of year, had a way of making the loss more prominent.

Karen counted her blessings any way she could, but this time of year was when she really felt Roy's absence. She felt it when she wrapped the presents; she felt it when she placed a wreath on his grave, and she felt it on a particular morning like this one.

It was 6am. The inky, winter darkness still consumed the outside and Karen was busy with the Christmas puddings and, of course, the Christmas cake. By tradition, she'd been lovingly feeding the cake and the puds for over a month now, trickling teaspoons of Roy's favourite brandy into the fruit-packed sponges every week. She was well known for perhaps being a little heavy-handed on the alcohol. But what was a Christmas treat without a little kick to it? She practically felt Roy's hand tilt the bottle for that extra splash.

'Don't be shy, maid. The boozier, the better.'

From the afternoon of Stir Up Sunday onward, Karen had felt the heaviness of Roy's absence creep in, as it always did. Seeing her darling Tom happy again, Sarah and Steve settled in their new marriage and having Mark back in regular contact again certainly made her look forward to Christmas this year, and yet she still found herself sighing melancholically as she peeled back the foil, releasing the boozy, citrus aroma.

She was startled as a plump little robin landed on the sill of the open window. It ruffled its feathers and gave a merry tweet.

'Hello, Roy my love,' Karen whispered to the red-breasted bird. It was a well-known fact that when a robin appears, a loved one is near. Karen had lived by that fact for many years, and it brought great comfort to her in times of needs.

She pulled out a small bag of seeds from under the sink and scattered a handful onto the sill. The robin hopped gaily over and pecked happily, offering a little tweet and a whistle in return.

Karen watched the robin for a long time, allowing her mind to wander. The year her dear husband passed away, she thought she'd never enjoy something like Christmas ever again. She couldn't say it had got easier over the years, but she'd found ways to adapt and appreciate the blessings in her life. This year, more than ever, she could count all three of her children to be the biggest blessing of all.

'Mum?'

The uncertainty in her daughter's voice caught Karen's attention. From a very young age, Sarah had always been confident and sure about everything she put herself to. So, when that voice was anything but strong, like now for instance, Karen was ready to catch her.

'What's the matter, my love?' Karen asked, closing the gap between them, and giving Sarah her undivided attention.

'I've got something to tell you,' Sarah began. 'But you have to promise not to lecture me or anything, because even though I feel like poop, I've realised I'm actually bloody happy about it so...'

Sarah's fumbling words were cut short as Karen gasped, her hands flying up to her mouth and her eyes brimming with tears. 'Oh! Oh, my love. That's wonderful.'

'I haven't told you what it is yet!' Sarah protested.

'Oh, you don't have to my love,' Karen said, gently. 'Call it a mother's instinct if you like, but it's an easy puzzle to work out. With the sickness, and the way you're holding your belly. Oh, that really is wonderful news.' She pulled her daughter into a tight hug and felt Sarah's shoulders sag in relief.

'It is, isn't it?' Sarah admitted, her voice small but happy. 'I really do feel like poop though. I don't think I've ever been so tired.'

'You're growing a human being... from scratch,' Karen reminded her. 'You're going to have to start taking it easy from now on. Thank goodness you have Emily with you in the tearoom now. I'm sure she and Poppy can work something out as you get bigger. I'm sure I have a crochet pattern for a lovely baby blanket. I'll make a start just as soon as I've finished that hat I was making for Emily.'

'Mum,' Sarah said. 'I need you to take it back a notch. I'm trying not to freak out here and you seem to have everything planned seconds from finding out.'

'Of course, my love. I'm just so delighted for you. And Steve?'

'Over the moon,' Sarah said, smiling. 'We're both in shock, actually. It's all happened so quickly!'

Karen chuckled wryly, wagging her finger. 'My love, it's in the genes. Your father only had to look at me in a certain way and I was pregnant.'

With that, Sarah's eyes darted vacantly to a spot on the wall just above her mother's head, her hands poised on Karen's shoulders as she pulled out of the hug. She patted them stiffly as Karen chuckled at her reaction.

'I did not need to know that mother. I did not need to know that.'

Three Days Until Christmas...

Tom tried not to think back to his short marriage with Catherine if he could help it. Self-preservation had a clever way of making sure that part of his memories got filed away, deep in a locked away compartment of his mind. But knowing she was only a stone's throw away from the safety of his farm made that self-preservation near impossible.

There had been a plethora of bangs, crashes, drilling, and shouts coming from The Old Riding School all morning, and Tom found himself watching the busy ongoings from the edge of the orchard which sat between the two properties. One hand deep in his pocket and the other clutching his coffee tightly, his face was in danger of freezing into the hard grimace that was currently in place on his weathered features.

Why did she have to be here?

The last few months, with Emily in his life, had made him realise just how much at peace he could be. Emily needed him and he needed her. He was happier that he could ever have imagined to be. But something was triggered yesterday, and all that closure he thought he had gained felt like it had vanished. He didn't think he was capable of being a possessive man, but his brother had done it once before... was he capable of taking Emily from him too? Deep down he knew it was an absurd thought, but that's where his mind was at right now. And he blamed Catherine's return entirely.

Tom knew that standing there in the bitter easterly wind wasn't going to help matters, so he finished the dregs of his coffee and headed towards his 4x4. He didn't have time for this. He had a turkey to pick up.

He closed his car door with a rattling thud and clicked his seatbelt into place, his hand poised over the key ignition just as Mark sprung out from nowhere, making Tom jump.

'Are you popping out?' Mark said, after he opened the passenger door and peered in.

'I'm picking up the turkey. Why?' Tom said, failing to hide the irritation in his voice.

'Mind if I join you?' Mark asked, though he didn't look particular keen on the idea himself.

Tom sighed and turned the ignition, his 4x4 roaring to life and settling into a loud purr. 'If you must.'

They were silent for the first ten minutes of the journey, but Tom knew exactly what was coming next.

'Thought we should talk,' Mark finally said, confirming Tom's suspicions. 'We haven't had a chance to talk, and I think you've got the wrong end of the stick with this whole Catherine ordeal.'

'Have I now,' Tom muttered, his eyes fixed to the road and his hands gripping the steering wheel.

'Emily was just as pissed at me for going to see her, but I only went down there to confront her – to tell her to leave you all alone. It took me by surprise to find that she had a sister and that she'd bought the riding school for her sister.' Mark blew hot breaths into his hands and started fiddling with the old thermostat. 'Does your heater even work in this old thing?'

'Wait – what? Catherine has a sister?' Had he been that inattentive as a husband that this little detail had slipped his memory?

'She's only known about her in the last year apparently,' Mark said, giving up on heating the cabin. 'Older sister, by about five years I think.'

Mark paused and Tom could feel his eyes on him for a moment. When Tom didn't say anything, this seemed to give Mark permission to continue.

'Her name is Grace. Remarkable lady, with Downs Syndrome. Completely independent. For all her flaws, Catherine is just trying to do right by her sister. Her parents chose not to raise Grace, and Catherine just wants to do right by her.'

Again, Tom said nothing. He processed this information and simply focused on his driving. The Land Rover finally pulled out from the long, bumpy lanes and onto the main road where the cabin was much quieter and smooth to sit in, and still Tom pondered for a little while longer.

'I'll give you the rest of the journey to take all that in,' Mark offered, pulling his phone out from his pocket, no doubt heading straight to his work emails. 'I'll run a little idea past you on the way home.'

When Tom finally returned to the warmth of his and Emily's little barn conversion that evening, the turkey now safely placed in his mother's kitchen ready for preparation, his heart warmed at the sight of his darling Emily in front of the fire, wrapping the last of their presents to the family.

'Thank god I have you to wrap the presents this year,' Tom remarked, placing his wax jacket around the back of the nearest chair. 'I'm bleddy useless at wrapping. Last year everyone received their presents in newspaper because I forgot all about it until Christmas Eve.'

'Well, that is a sorry state of affairs. How have you coped all these years?' Emily teased, receiving a kiss from Tom as he joined her on the floor with a bottle of cider.

'Poorly,' Tom confirmed, stoking the fire, and adding a log. His eyes popped in glee as he spotted a plate of Emily's homemade stollen. He pointed at them, seeking permission to help himself.

'Help yourself,' Emily said, distracted with the gift tag she was writing. 'We had quite a bit left over today.'

As Tom chewed on the deliciously sweet bread, noting the added marzipan flavour, he thought about

Mark's plan. It wasn't a bad plan, he reluctantly admitted that. But it would be one hell of an operation. Watching Emily as she wrote out gift tags, humming happily along to the gentle Christmas music playing in the background, he knew it wouldn't matter how big or difficult the plan was – he'd do anything for her.

Two Days Until Christmas...

The sun had barely risen, and the surrounding countryside looked hazy and indistinct. A thick fog still sat heavy above the freezing cold ground and dew drops threatened to freeze into sharp icicles. And yet, the tearoom at Trengrouse Cider Farm was fit to burst with Christmas songs, bellowing laughter and delighted squeals from children waiting in excited anticipation for the arrival of Father Christmas.

'Is it one sausage or two on each plate?' Mark asked, a tray of sausages balanced in one hand and tongs in the other. It was all hands-on deck in Sarah's tiny tearoom kitchen and even Mark had replaced the office suit for an apron to get stuck in.

'Adults two, children one,' Karen instructed, dishing out the fried eggs on each plate. 'Steve, my love - take these four plates to the family on table 3. This one is vegetarian.'

Steve did as instructed and passed through into the main customer area with the plates, where Emily and Poppy had a production line of hot drinks going. Tom was in the firing line, delivering them to the correct tables whilst dodging the paper airplanes that were flying across the tiny room.

It was Trengrouse Cider Farm's first Breakfast with Father Christmas, and it certainly wouldn't be their last. Emily and Poppy giggled in delight as crackers were pulled from all directions and a sing song began amongst the children for 'Jingle Bell Rock'. The little tearoom building really was far too small for this level of noise but everyone, from the children to the parents, seemed to be having a wonderful time.

'This is fantastic!' Emily shouted over the racket to Poppy, topping a cappuccino with some festive shimmery cocoa powder.

'What?!' Poppy shouted back, sprinkling a caramelized peanut hot chocolate with some chopped nuts.

'I said, this is fantastic!' Emily repeated.

Poppy looked more confused. 'Something about plastic?'

'Forget it!' Emily laughed, waving the conversation off. She was a little relieved when Steve and Mark started bringing out more plates, with more children tucking into their cooked breakfasts than belting out Christmas songs. Soon enough, it was only the Christmas track that could be heard, which Emily brought down to a much more low-key volume, and a happy murmur amongst the patrons as everyone finally had their breakfasts and a drink to enjoy.

Emily watched with satisfaction from behind the counter as Poppy started operation clean up, the usual explosion of cocoa powder, marshmallows and milk taking over.

'Thank god for that,' Tom said, looking frazzled and rubbing the side of his head. 'You'd think my head would be in safe range, being over 6ft.'

Emily smiled and snaked her arm through his, her head feeling a bit tight and weary despite her overloaded happiness.

'You're looking tired, sweetie,' Tom said gently. 'Why don't you go back to ours for a bit, have a drink and sit in peace? These children will be done eating in a minute and will be ready to scream out another Christmas number.' His face set in a hard grimace at the thought, but his eyes remained good humoured. Emily realised there and then that Tom had a lot more time and patience for children that he cared to admit. He was right though, the acoustics in this tiny little stone building was all wrong for ten mini, off-key carol singers and her head was beginning to throb. She kissed her fiancé gratefully on the cheek, told Poppy where she was going and peeled off her apron.

'In fact, take preggers with you,' Tom added. 'I'll send Poppy over with a hot chocolate for you both in a bit. You both deserve it after pulling all this off.'

'She's told you!' Emily cried, her hands clapping together in delight. She assessed his expression, having wondered how Sarah's eldest brother would react. 'And?'

'Brilliant news,' Tom smiled, his eyes twinkling. 'Now go...rest! I have Father Christmas to pick up from the distillery in the back of the trailer. Hoping he hasn't been doing any sampling over there whilst getting ready. All we need is for Father Christmas to be pissed as a fart!'

Breakfast with Father Christmas successfully executed, the man of the hour arriving jolly (and sober) not long after the breakfasts were enjoyed and devoured, the tearoom was closed for the rest of the day for operation Winter Wonderland to begin.

There was a lot to be done but, as always, many hands made for light work, and Trengrouse Cider Farm soon made its slow transition into a magical, Christmas haven. Even in the dimming daylight in mid-afternoon, the lights on the barns and giant Christmas tree in the yard looked spectacular.

'The hog roast guys have arrived. Where shall I put them?' Gary, one of the distillery men, asked Emily.

'Ask them to set up here, in the yard. The churros lady is going there and the roasted chestnut station here.'

'Right you are, Bird!' Gary said, happily. 'Did you know I'll be in the brass band later?'

'No! I didn't know you played!' Emily exclaimed, delighted.

Gary looked suddenly bashful but proud. 'Tenor horn. Father's on bass and Mother on cornet. Been a bit of a family affair for years. Even me wife will be shaking the jingle bells with the collection box.'

'I had no idea! I'll be sure to pull away from the tearoom sometime during the evening to watch you. By the way, have you seen Tom or Mark at all? They disappeared over an hour ago and I could do with Tom's height to install the lights over here.'

'No, haven't seen them. Hope they haven't killed each other,' Gary joked, though both he and Emily exchanged concerned looks. Tom and Mark probably shouldn't be left alone for too long, with their matching tempers. 'If I see either of them, I'll send them your way.'

'Thanks, Gary.'

Emily took a step back from the black board she had been writing on, the chalk pen poised in her hand as she assessed whether she needed to draw more snowflakes around the lettering 'Food Yard This Way!'. Deciding the snowflake ratio was fine, she turned and looked around in hopes of spotting Tom or Mark. There wasn't long to go until the public began to arrive and there was still so much to do. Where could they possibly be? Together?

Another hour passed and the Winterland Wonderland was almost complete. Emily, Sarah and Karen walked proudly around the yard which was quickly filling with the delicious, sweet concoction of roasted chestnuts and cinnamon sugared churros, mixed with the mouth-watering smell of the hog roast now rotating over a fire. Despite the darkness, the yard and surrounding barns were flooded in light from the abundance of twinkling lights.

'Oh, my loves! It's all looking spectacular!' Karen cried, her eyes glistening. Emily noted the wobble in her voice and hooked her arm around Karen's middle. 'You've really outdone yourselves. Roy would have loved this.'

'Oh, don't Mum! I'm bloody hormonal as it is,' Sarah wept, dabbing her eyes with the sleeve of her Christmas jumper. 'Whose idea was it to have a bloody hog roast?'

'Yours, my love,' Karen said, exchanging a knowing smile with Emily as Sarah held her delicate stomach, drawing in deep breaths.

'Anywhere I can be stationed where it doesn't smell of weird festive spices and meat?'

Emily glanced at the clipboard in her hand, which she'd been using to keep tabs on arriving stalls and food trucks. 'You can oversee the children's Christmas crafts in the main barn if you like.'

Sarah's deadpan expression hinted that she didn't like that idea very much. 'Screaming children and a shit load of glitter. Great.'

Karen and Emily chuckled as Sarah shuffled her way unenthusiastically towards the barn. Then Karen headed off to the tearoom ready to serve mince pies, stollen and other festive bakes. Emily studied her checklist for the umpteenth time and was about to check on the distillery boys who were stationed at the entrance to oversee the public parking, when Tom and Mark finally came into view, from the direction of the orchards.

'Where have you guys been?' Emily asked, trying to leave the irritation out of her tone. She was surprised to see them both looking very pleased with themselves. 'Why do I get the impression you have both been up to something?'

Tom and Mark exchanged mysterious looks and Tom gestured for Emily to follow him, holding his hand out to her. Despite her initial annoyance, Emily yielded and slipped her hand into Tom's, allowing herself to be led back towards the orchards. It was quickly apparent what they had been up to, and Emily audibly gasped in wonder at the sight before her.

Thousands of fairy lights adorned the apple trees, a guiding tunnel of sparkle, with glowing paper stars dotted sporadically in between. As Emily entered the magical tunnel, she realised how far it went and where it led to.

'This way, the public can flit between the two events,' Mark explained from behind them. 'Catherine agreed to it.'

'How did you convince her?' Emily asked, unable to peel her eyes away from the enchanting scene before her.

'She didn't have an alcohol licence or public liability insurance,' Tom scoffed, rolling his eyes up to the night's sky. 'Nothing's changed there. Couldn't organise a piss up in a brewery.'

'This must have taken you ages. You didn't surely do all of this in one afternoon.'

'No, we started it yesterday but ran out of lights,' Tom explained. 'B&Q and all the supermarkets within a ten-mile radius are completely sold out on solar panel fairy lights now, by the way.'

'Oh, my god!' Emily chuckled. 'It must have cost you a fortune! This tunnel has to be about half a kilometre long.'

'Mark paid,' Tom said, pointing behind him to Mark who was looking bashful, with his hands in his pockets.

'We can't let him pay for all this!' Emily protested.

'What's the point of having a rich brother?' Tom joked.

Mark nodded, agreeing in good humour. 'Fair point. It's on me, Em. Think of it as your Christmas bonus from Blake&Co.'

'Thank you,' Emily said to them both, her eyes dazzling in excitement. She took her phone from her back pocket and snapped a shot of the light tunnel trailing all the way through the orchard to the open gate leading to the riding school. She could just make out all the festivities coming to life on the other end. 'I'm going to post this on the Facebook Event page. Two Christmas Festivals for the price of one? We're going to be a sell out!'

Tom smiled; pride etched across his entire face. 'We have time. Fancy a tour of the lights?'

Mark took Emily's clipboard from her, encouraging her to 'take five' and heading off to check on the parking situation. Tom held his arm out and gathered Emily into his side before guiding her through the tunnel of lights.

The bright, melodic sound of the brass band playing 'Good King Wencelas' kicked off the evening less than an hour later, the yard filling fast with excited members of the public. Festive foods and spiced hot drinks were consumed in plenty, and there was a palpable merriness in the air.

The light tunnel was a hit and soon there was a steady traffic of people coming and going from both directions between Trengrouse Farm and The Old Riding School. Even Trengrouse Farm's Father Christmas joined forces with The Old Riding School's reindeer at one point in the evening, the children flocking to see them both in person.

Tom had been pulling pints all evening from the distillery, feeling absolutely ridiculous in the Santa hat which his silly sister had forced him to wear. But even he couldn't deny that the whole evening was a hit and that it got even him into the Christmas spirit. He listened with contentment as the brass band started on a round of Cornish carols, instantly recognising them from the years of his dear father belting them out this time of year. It had quietened down a bit in the food and drink areas whilst Father Christmas and the reindeer took up most of the attention, so Tom pulled his own pint and allowed the other lads to pick up the slack for a moment. Just as the brass band belted out the first verse of *Now the Holly Bears a Berry,* Tom wandered into the yard to observe the goings-on around the rest of the festival. He spotted his Emily through the open doors of the tearoom, looking as radiant as ever as she served a family their hot chocolates and festive bakes. He smiled as she and his mother chatted happily between them: he hadn't seen his mum look so happy in years. He thought about his sister and his best friend Steve, the both of them in their own bubble of joy as they adjusted to the idea of becoming parents. Tom was over the moon for them and knew that they would be the most fantastic parents together: Steve with his calm, patient nature and Sarah for her fun, explosive energy – at least, when she wasn't feeling sick. Then there was Mark. As infuriating and pretentious as he was sometimes, Tom was glad to see his little brother ditch the suit, the office and even the laptop to simply enjoy an evening of Christmas merriment, looking equally ridiculous in his own Santa hat as he helped with the clear up of glitter, glue and tinsel from the children's Christmas crafts workshop.

He was beginning to think it was the perfect evening. But his heart plummeted as he spotted her signature platinum curls bobbing through the busy crowd. A lady linked arms with her closely, about a foot smaller against Catherine's high heeled boots. She spotted Tom and faltered slightly before deciding otherwise and approaching him with confidence only Catherine could muster.

'If you want me to go, I'll go,' Catherine jumped straight in, recognising Tom's stature as an unwelcoming one. 'Grace wanted to see what was on the other end of the tunnel. Plus, your Santa nicked our Rudolf.'

Tom glanced at the small lady attached to Catherine's arm and eased his aggressive front. He smiled stiffly. 'Hi Grace. They're decorating gingerbread men in the tearoom in about fifteen minutes.'

'Yes! I love gingerbread men!' Grace exclaimed, heading straight for the tearoom without a second thought.

'I wish I had her ability to just decide something and go for it,' Catherine said conversationally, looking anywhere and everywhere but in Tom's direction.

'I don't know,' Tom muttered. 'You have a habit of deciding things and 'going for them'.'

Catherine's smile was a grimace. 'OK. Too soon for small talk. Umm, Grace is pretty self-efficient but just get her to text me when she's done, and I'll walk back up and get her.'

Tom nodded and promised to keep an eye on her. Catherine turned to go but paused for a moment before turning back to Tom.

'I'm glad you're happy. I mean that.' Catherine's words were so genuine that Tom couldn't even bring himself to scoff. 'Emily seems great. You two seem so much more suited for one another than we ever were.'

Catherine's words settled and a strange sort of peace came over Tom in that instance. He nodded, his words failing him.

'Merry Christmas, Tom.'

And with that, Catherine disappeared through the crowd and out of sight.

Christmas Eve...

It was the arrival of Christmas Eve and, with the tearoom closed and the farm shut to the public, by now Sarah would be in full holiday spirit, tucking into every edible Christmas treat she could get her hands on.

This year was clearly going to be different.

Sarah retched into the toilet, her stomach aching in protest. *Was it possible to get an RSI from something as repetitive as morning sickness?* Sarah thought to herself. She'd never felt so poorly in her life, and yet she rubbed her tummy with a fondness she didn't fully understand yet. She was going to be a mother. She wasn't sure whether she could be any happier if she tried.

Another wave of sickness and Sarah wretched once more into the toilet.

OK, she could probably be a little happier.

Nevertheless, it was Christmas Eve either way and Sarah was determined to give her future sister-in-law the merriest Trengrouse Christmas yet.

'Over there is where the Waters side of your family are buried. Great Aunty Cybil. Your great, great, Aunty Doris.' Karen placed a small holly wreath on one of the graves and proceeded to point out other areas of the cemetery where ancestors were laid to rest. Tom, Mark and Sarah all wore matching glazed expressions on their faces as they shuffled along behind their mother. Steve nodded politely, feigning interest, whilst Emily listened to Karen intently, in general awe of this little family history lesson.

'Your family is enormous! You're so lucky to know so much about where you came from,' Emily sighed, longingly.

Sarah's arms were folded tightly across her chest, and she wore a stony expression across her face. 'Yeah. This isn't the merry part of our Trengrouse Christmas I've been talking about.'

'Christmas is all about traditions,' Karen remarked, placing her last wreath down on the grave in front of her. 'And paying a visit to family graves... placing a wreath here and there... that's one of our traditions.'

'That, and getting pissed. But looks like I won't be doing that this year!' Sarah exclaimed. Karen relented and ushered them all in the direction of the cars, where her three adult children practically scampered back as fast as they could. Emily held back, linking arms with her future mother-in-law, and was quite content to take in the scenery on her return to the 4x4.

The rest of the day was reserved for eating, drinking and taking things slowly. It was the one time in the year where the Trengrouses were seen taking it easy.

It was now evening, and a very intense round of the Beetle Game was underway. Emily rolled the dice and her hands shot up in the air in triumph.

'Yes! Three! Pass me a blue antenna,' Emily instructed, holding her hand out to Steve who had the box of beetle parts. 'Just an eye and a front leg to go.'

'How is the newbie winning?' Sarah complained. 'I haven't even got my head yet!' She rolled the dice, then passed it over to Tom in a huff.

Tom rattled the dice in his closed hand, taking a swig of his drink with another. 'Looks like Mum's on her way to winning. Steve mate, pass me a yellow eye.'

'Do you know... I think it's going to snow tonight,' Emily shared with the table, her cheeks a little blushed from the excess wine and heat from the AGA. Everyone chortled around the table in disbelief. 'It's the perfect conditions for it. It's freezing out there.'

'We don't get white Christmases in Cornwall,' Tom said. 'You'll be lucky to get hail.'

'Well, I reckon it will,' Emily said, stubbornly.

'Oh, oh!' Karen cried, her hands waving about in excitement. 'Bee- Bee... Bingo Bango Bongo!'

The whole room collapsed into fits of laughter as Karen presented her completed plastic beetle proudly, helping herself to a refill of the wine in celebration.

'It's Beetle, Mum!' Sarah cried, laughing hysterically.

Something beeped on the kitchen counter and Steve practically jumped out of his seat. He lifted the lid off Karen's giant slow cooker and rubbed his hands gleefully.

'It's ready! It's ready!' Steve exclaimed, getting utensils out and setting a large serving plate on the counter.

'Oh, that smells delicious Steve,' Karen said, getting up and peering into the slow cooker. 'Oh, well done you!'

Everybody waited in hungry anticipation as Steve heaved the enormous gammon hock onto the serving plate, admiring it proudly.

'This has been cooking slowly all day. Honey and marmalade-glazed and marinated in the best cider in Cornwall – obviously!'

Everybody groaned in appreciation and suddenly everyone was up, all hands-on deck to lay the table ready for supper. In less than ten minutes, the large kitchen table was adorned with warm rolls, cheeses of every kind, pigs in blankets, cold meats, pickles, potatoes, and of course Steve's gammon masterpiece, taking centre stage. It was a feast fit for kings and soon everybody was tucking in. Even Sarah tentatively picked and nibbled on whatever her stomach allowed her to have.

'Merry Christmas, everyone!' Mark announced, his wine glass held up in thanks.

Everyone raised their glasses and a chorus of 'Merry Christmas' bounced around the four warm walls of Karen's country kitchen.

Christmas Day

A glittery diamond trail of sun gleamed through a gap in the curtains, and Emily began to stir from its radiance. She smiled as her thoughts trailed off to last night, an evening of music, games, food and cheer. Her smile widened further as she turned around to find Tom sound asleep next to her, his dark eyelashes creating shadows and his features softened from a peaceful slumber. Emily suddenly realised this was the first time she'd woken to Tom sound asleep. Usually, he was awake by 5am and out on the farm to start an honest day's work. She ran a delicate hand down his face, feeling the gentle brush of his beard on her palm just as he showed the first signs of waking, his deep brown eyes focusing on her bottle greens.

'Good morning.' Tom smiled, his voice low and thick from sleep. 'What time is it?'

'It's almost eight,' Emily purred, running her hand through his hair. 'Think this might be the latest you've ever slept in.'

'Christ, half the day's gone,' Tom joked, heaving himself into a sitting position and kissing her softly on the cheek. 'Merry Christmas, sweetheart.'

Tom's lips migrated to Emily's lips, his fingers trailing into her hair as he deepened his kiss. They were about to progress to much more physical things when there was a frenzied knock on their front door.

'Emily! Emily, come quick!' Mark's voice could be heard from downstairs, his frantic banging causing them both to startle. 'You'll never believe it! Quick, get down here before it all melts!'

Emily gasped, practically hurling herself out of bed. 'It snowed! I knew it – it snowed!'

Tom sighed in disappointment and climbed out of bed, following his feverish fiancée down the stairs. Emily yanked the door open and joined Mark into the yard, ready to see the farm in a blanket of snow.

'Where... ?' Emily looked in all directions. 'Where's the snow?'

'Over here,' Mark said, gesturing for Emily to follow him as Tom took a pew on the nearest bench, looking somewhat bored. Mark led Emily to a patch of brownish, white sludge and erupted into a wave of laughter. 'There's your Cornish white Christmas, Em! A nice little pile of sleet.'

'Thanks,' Emily muttered. 'You're hilarious. Merry bloody Christmas!'

Mark's mirth increased a notch as Emily stormed back inside. He shouted after her, 'you're turning British, Em! You sounded like Sarah then! Oh, come on Tom – it was funny!'

'You cock-blocked me for sleet,' Tom said, his expression stony which only made Mark laugh more. 'Dick.'

Mark's chuckles could be heard all the way back to the main house as Tom shut the door and found Emily staring at their tree, her body still.

'Do you want me to run him over with my Land Rover?' Tom joked, placing his warms hands on her dainty shoulders. 'Come on, babe. It was only a joke.'

'Where did these come from?' Emily asked, her voice thick and wobbly.

Tom followed her line of vision and saw the two red sacks sat fat and full under the Christmas tree. 'Oh, that's just our Santa sacks. Yes, I'm thirty-five years old, and yes I still get a Santa sack.'

'This one has my name on it.' Emily whispered, her fingers running across the green felted letters. 'Did Karen make these?'

'Yeah, we all have one,' Tom said, filling the kettle up and clicking it on for the first coffee of the day. 'Sarah,

Mark, Steve – we all have one. Even Dad had one. Aw, sweetheart – are you crying?'

He enveloped her in his arms and kissed the top of her head. Wiping her eyes with her sleeve, she dived straight into the sack to assess the contents.

'Your mother is the kindest woman I know,' Emily said, her smile reaching her twinkling green eyes. 'Oh, my god! Christmas socks!'

'I'd like to make a small announcement,' Mark said, after tinging his knife delicately against his prosecco and standing to attention.

The kitchen table was bursting with plates of roasted vegetables, crispy potatoes, and enormous Yorkshire puddings, all the Christmas trimmings dotted in between, from pigs in blankets to a large bowl of stuffing. Tom had begun to carve the turkey, dishing out slices of mouth-watering meat to the plates Karen held out ready.

'As you know, I was finally made partner recently at Blake&Co.'

'As if we could forget,' Steve muttered, receiving a dig to the ribs as Sarah shushed him.

'Well, the benefits of being partner is being able to base yourself wherever you choose,' Mark said, pausing for dramatic effect. 'The London branch is off to a flying start, so in the new year I will be taking charge of a second UK office... in Manchester.'

'You're moving back to the UK?' Karen asked, her hands trembling in anticipation in front of her face.

Mark nodded his confirmation. 'I secured a lease on an apartment in the city centre a couple of days ago.'

There was an eruption of happy squeals as both Karen and Sarah jumped to their feet, negotiating people and chairs to embrace Mark in happy hugs. Emily followed quickly after, congratulating him, and embracing him warmly. Even Tom and Steve squeezed his hand and patted his back in praise.

'Oh! What a wonderful Christmas this is turning out to be!' Karen cried, her eyes filling again.

'Oh, bleddy hell, you've set mother off,' Sarah teased, rolling her eyes as they all grabbed a glass of their chosen Christmas drinks to raise.

'I know you all think I'm just your silly, soppy mother. But seeing you all grow up to be such strong, accomplished, wonderful adults – well, it's enough to make a parent proud as punch. Your father would be so proud.'

There was a moment of silence as they all thought of Roy, a hundred memories circulating between them.

'So many things to look forward to,' Karen continued, her eyes swimming. 'Let's raise a toast to future events.' Six glasses were raised in the air. 'To Sarah and Steve – you're going to be wonderful parents my loves.'

Six glasses clinked and a babble of cheers and congratulations echoed around the room.

'To Mark, I'm so very happy to be having you back on this side of the Atlantic. And I'm so proud of everything you have achieved.'

More clinking and a murmur of agreement. Despite himself, Mark blushed, muttering 'thanks, mum.'

'And to the next newlyweds,' Karen finalised, her eyes twinkling at Tom and Emily. 'We'd best get cracking with wedding plans!'

'Not to make this about me...' Sarah butted in.

'Wouldn't be like you, sis,' Tom jeered, his eyes rolling to the ceiling.

'...but can you wait until I've had the baby. I don't want to be fat in all your wedding photos.'

Karen tutted and scolded whilst everyone else chuckled knowingly at Sarah's ways. The glasses clinked one more time and the room fell into contentment as everyone tucked into Karen's delicious Christmas roast.

Emily's eyes scanned the table, taking in all the love and joy. Her heart was full. Karen was right, there was so much to look forward to, and she couldn't wait for it all to begin.

The End

About the Author

Lamorna Ireland

A proper Cornish maid with a rich Cornish heritage, Lamorna Ireland has taken inspiration from the beautiful county from a very young age. Whilst teaching English in a local secondary school and being a dedicated wife and mother, Lamorna has always taken joy from the written word. In April 2020, she released her debut novel, 'Unexpected Beginnings' – a contemporary romance set on a Cornish cider farm, which tells the story of a young American girl finding unexpected beginnings under the nurturing wing of the Trengrouse family. The story gives an insight to the complicated tangles of family love and grief, whilst transporting readers to the tranquil Cornish countryside. In April 2021, Lamorna released her second Cornish-set romance, 'Unexpected Truths' - set in the thriving fishing village, Mevagissey.

Lamorna's love for coffee and quality food has recently inspired her to write a blog for some of her favourite tearooms and cafés, whilst taking her debut novel on its own unique book tour. Her blog Lamorna Corner can be found bursting with positive vibes and yummy places to visit, including The Elm Tree tearooms and Duchy of Cornwall Nursery.

Lamorna continues to spend her free time adventuring around her beautiful home county, her feet firmly rooted to the place of her ancestors.

You can follow the latest news and updates on Lamorna's work on her website (www.lamornaireland.co.uk), as well as Facebook, Twitter and Instagram. She also sends out a quarterly newsletter with exclusive news for her VIP readers, which is free to subscribe to.

Printed in Great Britain
by Amazon

87556127R00047